THINK YOU CAN HANDLE
JAMIE KELLY'S FIRST YEAR OF DIARIES?

AND DON'T MISS YEAR TWO!

Jim Benton's Tales from Mackerel Middle School

DEAR DUMB DIARY,

MY PANTS ARE HAUNTED!

BY JAMIE KELLY

SCHOLASTIC INC.

ISBN 978-0-439-62905-8

40 39 38 37   19 20/0
Printed in the U.S.A.   40
First printing, October 2004

For
the misunderstood.

Special thanks to:
Julie Kane-Ritsch and Carole Postal
along with all the punks at Scholastic, including:
Martha Atwater, Maria Barbo, Steve Scott,
Susan Jeffers Casel, and Shannon Penney.

THIS DIARY PROPERTY OF

Jamie Kelly

SCHOOL: MACKEREL MIDDLE SCHOOL

LOCKER: 101

Best friend: Isabella

Pet: Stinker (beagle)

Occupation: FASHION expert and makeover guru

READ NO FURTHER

UNLESS you are me,

I command you to Stop reading now.

if you are me,
sorry, it's cool

Dear Whoever Is Reading My Dumb Diary,

Are you sure you're supposed to be reading somebody else's diary? Have you done this before? If I did not give YOU permission, YOU had better stop right now. If you are my parents, then YES, I know that I am not allowed to call people idiots and fools and goons and half-wits and gerds and all that, but this is a diary, and I didn't actually "call" them anything. I *wrote* it. And if you punish me for it, then I will know that you read my diary, which I am *not* giving you permission to do.

Now, by the power vested in me, I do promise that everything in this diary is true, or at least as true as I think it needs to be.

Signed,

Jamie Kelly

PS: If this is you, Angeline, reading this, then you are officially busted. I happen to have this entire room under hidden video surveillance. And, in just a moment, little doors will slide open and flesh-eating rats will stream into the room. And, like tiny venomous cowboys, scorpions will be riding the rats. So it's curtains for you, Angeline! Mwah-hah-hah-hah!

PSS: If this is you, Margaret or Sally, then HA-HA — you are also caught in my surveillance sting.

Dear Jamie-
I am so sure. I
do NOT read your diary.
So get over yourself.

-Isabella

PS- I totally agree with
the stuff you said
about your mom.

Sunday 01

Dear Dumb Diary,

   Mom and I got into a "discussion" about fashion after dinner tonight. Of course, she really has no idea what the trends are at my school. I told her that I think she can't possibly know how important trends can be, and she said that clothes were just as important when she was in middle school. Then I said that I understood how she probably always tried her best to make a good impression on Fred and Wilma and Barney and the whole gang down at the tar pit, but times had changed.

a typical mother-daughter discussion

And that's just part of the reason I'm here in my room way ahead of schedule for the evening. Here's the exchange that followed my Mom-Is-Old-As-Cavemen joke:

"Just how do you think that makes me feel?" Mom asked.

"Stupid?" I guessed.

MOST DANGEROUS THINGS ON EARTH

BEAR THAT CAN BURP UP HAND GRENADES

GIANT SHARK WITH LITTLE SHARKS FOR TEETH

MY MOM WHEN YOU'RE TRYING TO MAKE HER ANGRY

Turns out that Mom had a different answer in mind, and I'll have a little time to figure out what it was since I'm here in my bedroom about five hours earlier than usual.

I also think that Dad sitting there trying *not* to laugh might have made things worse.

You can always tell when Dad is trying not to laugh

Sometimes diaries can be so much easier to talk to than moms. I can't picture Mom letting me write on her face, and I imagine sliding a bookmark in somewhere would result in a major wrestling match.

Monday 02

Dear Dumb Diary,

Angeline is back to her old tricks, Dumb Diary.

Yeah, sure, for a long time, everything was fine between us. (Nearly four whole days — except two of those were over the weekend, during which I did not see her.) But then today, in science class, while I was talking to Hudson Rivers (eighth cutest guy in my grade), she performed an act of **UTTER BEAUTY** and distracted him.

Actually, I hadn't started to talk to him yet, but I was going to, and she should have known that when she whipped out her **GORGEOUSNESS** and waved it all over the place.

Isn't it time we stopped the beautiful people?

It's true. I may not be fully qualified to talk to Hudson Rivers. Maybe he *is* just slightly too cute for me. (I'm right on the edge of adorable.) But if I'm really, really lucky and keep my fingers crossed, he could become mildly disfigured. Then we'd be on the same level, and I want to make sure I'm ready should that blessed maiming occur.

A Beautiful thought
you are just one Rampaging Elephant away from marrying the Handsomest Boy in the school

And besides, Angeline is in that Mega-Popular category where she can probably go and work her wicked charms against boys like Chip, who is the number one cutest boy in the school.

So why does she always have to perform acts of **Beauty** around Hudson?

(Chip, like Madonna and Cher and Moses, only goes by his first name. I'm not sure anybody knows what his last name is.)

other one-Namers

PINK

TARZAN

BEEPY

THE SCIENCE OF BOY-OLOGY
Local Specimens

CHIP
CUTENESS RANKING: **1**
NON-MEAN AND HANDSOME ENOUGH TO BE IN A SHAVING CREAM COMMERCIAL

HUDSON RIVERS
CUTENESS RANKING: **8**
EASILY TRICKED INTO THINKING ANGELINE IS PRETTY. OTHERWISE EXCELLENT

ROSCO
(CHIP'S DOG)
CUTENESS RANKING: **19**
STRICTLY SPEAKING NOT A BOY, BUT CUTER AND WAY MORE POPULAR THAN MOST TRUE BOYS

MIKE PINSETTI
CUTENESS RANKING: **ALMOST LAST**
MEAN AND MOUTHY. IF YOU MEET HIM TELL HIM ALL ABOUT SOAP.

THAT ONE KID
CUTENESS RANKING: **LAST**
DOES HE EVEN HAVE A NAME? WHO KNOWS. HE DOESN'T SEEM TO NEED ONE

Tuesday 03

Dear Dumb Diary,

    Isabella came by after school to root through my magazines for those little paper perfume samples. She's got a top secret fragrance project she's working on. It's connected to her ongoing obsession with **Popularity,** I'm sure of it. Isabella is kind of an expert on Popularity, or so she says. (I know: Isabella belongs in a cage. But she is my best friend, **So One Does What One Must.**)

    I looked everywhere before I finally found my magazines. Get this: they were in my parents' room. Hmmm! Looked like Mom had been flipping through them. I wonder if she's planning to do some sort of makeover on herself.

AN EXCELLENT MOM MAKEOVER

I heard about this girl whose mom had a makeover done on herself, and it was so good that afterward the mom looked younger and hotter than the daughter, which made her feel so guilty that she decided to have the makeover unmade. But when the cosmetologists tried to undo what had been done, they said that her body had absorbed the makeover, and now she was permanently afflicted with **Hotness.**

So her daughter came down with a form of **Embarrassment** that has to be treated by doctors.

I've never seen anything like it, nurse. This girl's mom actually embarrassed her daughter's butt off.

Honestly, I'm not terribly worried about Mom having a makeover. She can hardly makeover a bed.

mom makes a bed

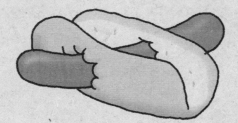

mom makes a hot dog

Wednesday 04

Dear Dumb Diary,

Here are what some people think are the worst things about my school:

When the Bus Drivers dress up for Halloween

Yo Dawgs— who's ready for some straight up Algebrizzle?

The unmistakable tangy flavor of horse organs in the cafeteria meatloaf.

When the teachers try talking cool

But they're wrong...

The worst thing about school is my science class. I like the *idea* of science. I mean, it comforts me to know that Angeline's guts are no more glorious or appealing than the stuff you'd scoop out of a porcupine.

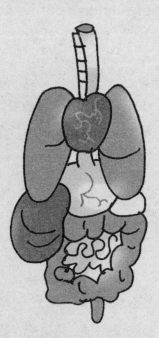

porcupine
guts

pretty girl
guts

you decide

But it's the whole chemistry part of it that I hate, like "this-kind-of-stuff-can-burn-through-this-junk," and "when-you-mix-this-with-that-then-whatever-will-explode." Science just doesn't seem to have much to do with what I'm trying to accomplish in my life right now, which is mainly the avoidance of science.

Are they even sure they want me in science class?

BOOM

At least Hudson Rivers is in my class. Isabella and I sometimes exchange scientific observations on Hudson.

Specimen chews gum at a rate of 32 chomps per minute

Specimen's right eye is 8% cuter than left eye

Specimen becomes mildly creeped out when it notices somebody counting its gum chews

Thursday 05

Dear Dumb Diary,

    Tonight at dinner I realized that I am, once again, the youngest person in my family. My beagle, Stinker, was once younger than me, but by employing the totally unfair dog trick of aging seven years in just twelve months, Stinker went from peeing on the carpet to being old enough to drive in just a couple years. He is the only member of my family who has ever accomplished such an amazing feat, except I think I have an uncle who might have done it, too.

    It is for this reason that I decided not to give Stinker my table scraps after dinner this evening. (Not because my uncle peed, but because Stinker made me the baby of the family *again*.)

Beagle actually trying to age 7 times faster than me.

This really made Stinker mad. Tonight, dinner was Chinese food — almost a beagle's favorite meal. (I wonder what they call Chinese food in China. They probably just say, "Here. Here's some of that food we always have.")

Friday 06

Dear Dumb Diary,

The vengeful beagle strikes again. To get back at me for not giving him my table scraps, Stinker ate a huge hole out of the backside of my only clean pair of jeans. (The second-best pair in the collection.) I know he would say he had to do it because he was so hungry from not having his normal gut-full of table scraps, but I know that he did it out of revenge.

How can I be so sure Stinker made the hole? It was in the most embarrassing place possible and it was **PERFECTLY** round. It looked like a tailor had chewed it.

Tailors are clothing experts and could probably bite a hole of any shape

So, I had to go with a pair of khaki pants that really had no business being out on a Friday. They're a Sunday pair of khakis. Sure, they started as a Friday pair of pants, but as cooler pants were purchased, the khakis were demoted.

I paired them with a shirt that was a *serious* Friday shirt, hoping to boost the khakis' confidence and give them the feeling that maybe they were somehow becoming more fashionable. It totally worked, of course, as pants are really stupid. You would think that a pair of khakis would notice that, currently, the most popular pants at my school are jeans, faded to just the right shade of blue.

PHASES IN THE LIFE OF PANTS

PHASE 1
Brand new and in style. Happiest time in a pant's life. Wear at any time.

PHASE 2
Slightly out of style or with taco stain. Wear on Sundays only.

PHASE 3
Hole bitten out of fanny by dog or tailor. Wear only as part of Hobo costume.

Of course, I don't *have* any jeans that are the perfect shade of blue. If I awoke one morning to discover that I had a pair that WAS the right shade of blue, I would just assume that they weren't my pants, it wasn't my house, and it wasn't me who had just woken up.

Other signals that could have indicated I was in the wrong house...

Dad encourages massive make-up abuse

Dog is not mean and spends several minutes a day not licking itself

Mom prepares a honstinking casserole which family voluntarily eats

Saturday 07

Dear Dumb Diary,

The most incredible thing happened today. Isabella and I saw Angeline, but not at school. It's always so weird when you know somebody only from school, but then you see them in the real world. It's like when you walk in on a clown, and he's only wearing his underpants. (Long story: Bad birthday party experience. Don't like clowns anymore.)

Anyway, Angeline was in the park, and she was playing with these two little kids who Isabella and I figured were her little sisters. But the little sisters did not have Angeline's great looks (**Nobody cares anyway, Angeline!**), thereby verifying what we have always just suspected about Angeline: **SHE'S BEEN PLASTIC-SURGEONED.** Probably nothing on her is an original part.

It would cost a fortune to do that much plastic surgery on somebody who started out as ugly as we hope Angeline did, so we figure that Angeline's dad is some big doctor.

On top of everything else, she's probably **RICH.**

ANALYSIS of THE Surgery they probably did on ANGELINE

HORN REMOVAL $1500

HAIR DYED AND MADE PERMANENTLY GOOD SMELLING $1800

CONTACT LENSES $800

NOSE JOB $4200

WING TRIM $2000

FANGECTOMY $1800

TAIL CUT OFF

EXTREME MANICURE $47

KNEES DE-KNOBBED

FEET PROBABLY LEFT THE SAME

Just when I thought I knew everything there was about Angeline that bugged me, it turns out she's also loaded.

Angeline taking a BATH IN PURE MONEY

Jewel encrusted soap

HOT AND COLD RUNNING DIAMONDS

RUG OF EXTRAORDINARY FLUFFINESS

Sunday 08

Dear Dumb Diary,

It's Sunday. Also known as **Homework Day**. Every weekend I tell myself that I'm going to finish my homework when I get home on Friday afternoon, and then I tell myself I'm going to do it Saturday morning, and then I tell myself I'll do it Saturday night, and then I tell myself to get off my back, and why am I always nagging myself, and then I call myself a name and have to apologize to myself.

And then I have to do all my homework on Sunday.

Tomorrow is school and I can't risk another wardrobe-munching by Stinker, so I gave him table scraps from dinner.

How Beagles enjoy their scraps

Sniff suspiciously for eleven minutes

SNIFF
SNURF
SNURF
SNIFF

cautiously pick up with front teeth

PINCE

Hork it down in one gulp and choke to death a little

GWARF
ACK
GAG
GULP

Monday 09

Dear Dumb Diary,

Okay. Who wants to buy a beagle cheap? Remember the other night we had Chinese food? Stinker didn't get any scraps and that's why he ate my pants.

Last night I gave him scraps, but Mom had cooked some sort of **Goo Casserole** and it had somehow slipped my mind that few living things except bacteria enjoy my mom's cooking. (Mom is a good mom and everything, but she's not very good at traditional mom things, like cooking and cleaning and washing clothes.) So *guess* what Stinker did?

pure love and joy →

utter disgust ↓

It looks like Stinker quietly crept through the house, carefully sorted through the laundry Mom had just done, found the absolute **best**-looking pair of jeans I own, and ate an even bigger hole. Through the front this time!

↑
pure
evil

Does anybody **know** why dogs do the things they do? I think they might do some of them (like *you-know-what*) just to see if they can get their picture in the newspaper for being the **GROSSEST DOG ON EARTH.** But why Stinker is gnawing through my pants is anybody's guess.

The Daily News

DOG DOES GROSSEST THING ANYBODY EVER HEARD OF

"SO DID WE" CLAIM OTHER LOCAL DOGS

The couch it happened behind

I could propose the question in science class, except it would draw attention to my pants and I had to wear khakis again today.

Our science class works like this: Everybody has a lab partner. A lab partner is a person that you do all the experiments with while you both wish the other one was Sally Winthorpe, who is this really smart girl who probably has a brain for every single organ in her body, because she's sort of tiny and her head is just not big enough to fit that much smartness in. Although I'm not sure what being that smart can get you.

Sally was Isabella's partner for a long time, but then they got switched. Of course now she's Angeline's partner, so I'm sure Angeline never has to do any work. Which, added to the whole being loaded thing, really kind of bites.

BLAH BLAH BLAH

BLAH BLAH BLAH

SALLY LISTENS

Isabella talked too much and Palmer switched them

For now my lab partner is Isabella — whose head is plenty big — but there's a chance she's using part of it for a lunch box or laundry hamper. She has been conducting this top secret science experiment involving collecting every single one of those perfume sample cards that they put in magazines, and combining them into one massive **SUPERFRAGRANCE** that she says will smell as good as every known good smell in the Universe, combined. She has been doing this in science class because she already has about seventy of them crammed in an old baby food jar she's kept hidden in a cabinet in the science room. Just taking the lid off the thing to stuff another one in requires her to wear the science class safety glasses.

Isabella has been having a sinus problem, so she can hardly smell at all. But without the glasses, she says the vapor could still blind her for life.

Angeline and her genius partner, Sally, spotted us doing a perfume deposit today. Angeline, though beautiful and therefore fundamentally evil, didn't tattle. Call her **conceited**. Call her **stuck-up**. Call her **self-centered**. I mean it. Somebody go get the phone and call her.

But the truth is that she could have squealed but didn't. My theory is that at Angeline's lofty level of **MEGA-POPULARITY,** a snitcher is frowned upon. (At one point I thought I might have even seen her smile a little, but I've seen crocodiles do the same thing, so I can't be sure what it means.)

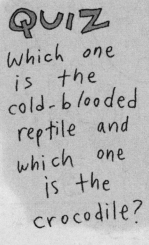

QUIZ
Which one is the cold-blooded reptile and which one is the crocodile?

Tuesday 10

Dear Dumb Diary,

    Isabella's sinus problem is still bugging her. She can't smell **anything**. She says her sinuses are bad enough that she could park in handicapped spaces if she were old enough to drive. Since she isn't, she says that the law allows her to just stand in them.

Wednesday 11

Dear Dumb Diary,

Isabella needed to make another perfume deposit today. I stood in front of her so that Mrs. Palmer, the science teacher, couldn't see what we were doing. (Mrs. Palmer replaced our previous teacher, Mr. Tweeds, who fell and broke his hip, which is what all old people do sooner or later because their skeletons are as brittle and cracky as pretzel rods. He's like 48 or something.) But it turns out that Mrs. Palmer, like most adults, doesn't really care **exactly** what you're doing when you are doing something that you're trying to hide. (Adults are like frogs that snap bugs out of the air without first getting a good look at them: Could be a butterfly. Could be a killer bee.) So Mrs. Palmer just separated us as lab partners.

Mrs. Palmer believes that switching partners whenever there is a problem is a good idea. Until today, I never believed her.

Mrs. Palmer is a teacher so naturally I assumed she would never do anything good for me. But...

You know how I said that adults are like frogs? Here's another aspect of their froggishness: Frogs are sometimes princes deep down inside. Or princesses, in Mrs. Palmer's case. (Although this particular princess would need a queen-size throne for **Her Royal Hineyness**.)

Mrs. Palmer had to split up another set of lab partners in order to separate Isabella and me. Sure, she *could* have paired me up with Margaret Parker, total reject. But she didn't. Dear, sweet Mrs. Palmer presented to me, like a humongous plate of cookies, my new lab partner, **HUDSON RIVERS**. She gave Hudson's old partner, Margaret Parker, to Isabella, like a plate of wet socks.

Don't get me wrong, Dumb Diary, Margaret is okay, I guess. She's kind of nice, but she's a **pencil chewer,** and most non-beavers find that a bit repulsive. (Isabella says that Margaret is a "GERD," which is a GIRL NERD.)

Isabella's Terms for Girls

GERD
(GIRL NERD)

MORONICA
(FeMALE IDIOT)

CHOCK
(chick jock)

COW
(WOMAN BULL)

Isabella used the opportunity to share with me (*again*) more about her theories on Popularity. She says that Unpopularity is contagious, and you can catch it the same way you catch the **Flu** or **Bad Dancing.** Honestly, though, I don't believe that Unpopularity is a real Force of Nature, like Gravity or Deliciousness. I told her that she should be more open-minded about her new partner. And that deep down inside, Margaret is probably a good person.

Then I realized what a beautiful and sensitive thing I had said, and I imagined that maybe one day I might open a big sanctuary where all the **Social Rejects** could live and run free and never have to worry about wedgies again. Plus, I could sell tickets to people to come and look at them.

Little Billy feeds one of my captive rejects its favorite snack

Thursday 12, 3:45 AM

Dear Dumb Diary,

I can't believe I stayed up this late. It's like, the middle of the night. There was this scary movie on TV tonight about this little girl who finds this old doll that's haunted, which anybody could tell was going to be haunted because she was a really sweet girl, and she really loved the doll, and there is just no way a movie is going to let a sweet little girl be happy with her doll. Not if it's a good movie, anyway.

But now I am in serious trouble because I still have science homework to finish and I blame my mom who is the one who let me have this TV in my room after I begged two years nonstop for it. (I mean, a kid can't spoil herself, Dumb Diary, am I right? My spoilage is Mom's fault.)

I'd like to write more, but I'm really tired and I have to get this homework finished.

If I don't, Mrs. Palmer is going to bite my

Friday 13

Dear Dumb Diary,

    That's right. I fell asleep last night without finishing my science homework. Which means, as predicted, that Mrs. Palmer bit my head off. And then it got worse. Figuring that the problem was with the new lab partner arrangement, she switched Hudson with Margaret. Now Margaret is my lab partner, and Isabella has Hudson.

Symptoms of Hudson Withdrawal
(exhibited ONLY in private)

And since I missed the homework, Mrs. Palmer suggested that Margaret and I get together over the weekend to get me caught up. And Margaret said, right there in front of many Popular ears, between munchy chomps on a damp pencil, "Great. What time should I come over, Jamie?"

If I had been less tired, and outfitted in more confident clothing (thanks, Stinker), I might have come up with a cool comeback. Maybe the coolest one ever, but now we'll never know because I sleepily said, "whenever," and Mike Pinsetti, who used to be in the business of making up nicknames for people, but is currently experimenting with other forms of annoying harassment, made a loud kissy-kissy sound. As most people know, in some parts of the world, the kissy-kissy sound of a bully is enough to actually legally marry two people to each other.

In this case, it suggested that perhaps Margaret and I were now best friends, and I could feel the Popularity flying off me like the delicate petals of a beautiful flower that somebody had stuck into the spinning blades of a fan.

Afterward, of course, Isabella didn't miss the opportunity to point out that I should be more open-minded about my new lab partner. I told her that open-minded is what you are if you get hit in the head with an ax, and I felt plenty open-minded enough.

Anyway, Dumb Diary, Margaret is coming over tomorrow.

Saturday 14

Dear Dumb Diary,

As foretold, Margaret came over. We finished the homework junk, and I realized that even though at first I had thought that Margaret was sort of an Unpopular Goof, after I got to know her a little, I realized that deep down, she was much worse than that.

often the inner person is way grosser

If there was anything to this Unpopularity infection thing, I was in serious trouble.

Fortunately, Isabella stopped by and we had a minute to talk privately while Margaret was in the bathroom, doing whatever it is that Unpopular people do in there. (Make themselves LESS presentable?)

The secret products of The UNPOPULAR

Love my Tangles™
HAIR UNCONDITIONER

Pork-color contact lenses

Horse Choker
STEW-SCENTED DEODORANT

Isabella had stopped by out of concern. She was concerned about her jar of SuperFragrance, which was gone, probably found by Mrs. Palmer. She was concerned that her lab partnership with Hudson didn't bother me enough. I assured her that it did, but since she was my best friend, I decided not to dwell on it. And she was most concerned that Margaret could drag down my Popularity, and since I'm friends with Isabella, it could affect her Popularity as well.

But Isabella had the solution. . . .

And it was an excellent one:
A MAKEOVER.

MAKEOVER PATIENT
PRIOR TO PROCEDURES

HUMP REMOVAL AND
RELOCATION

FULL BODY SHAVE

NOSE JOB

TAIL REMOVAL

EARS MOVED

NEW HAIR AND MAKEUP

PERFUME

HUMPS SEWN BACK ON

GLAMOROUS WARDROBE

EXPENSIVE SHOES

SPINE STRAIGHTENED

See? Makeovers totally work!

Just like on TV. We will help Margaret fix herself up a little, and thereby undo whatever damage she has done to us. Like all of our plans, this is surely a great idea.

Other great ideas of ours

the 9-foot-long french fry

some kind of pill you could take and be instantly healthy

the 18-foot-long french fry

I was trying to figure out a delicate way to suggest the makeover, but Isabella had already come up with a gentle way to introduce the idea to Margaret.

Margaret did not take this as hard as you might think. She seemed kind of sickly grateful for the attention. I felt a little bad and might have pulled out right there, except for how much fun it is to put makeup on somebody else's face. Tomorrow, Isabella and I, **Known Experts on Fashion**, will begin PROJECT MARGARET.

My Incredible Makeup Skills at Work

Frankenstein

The Mummy

Wolfman

Sunday 15

Dear Dumb Diary,

Project Margaret begins.

Amazingly, Mom was totally okay with taking us all to the mall today. I was fully prepared for a huge argument, followed by some crying, an apology, and finally, a trip to the mall. Mom's saying yes right away saved me about four minutes.

I had saved up a LOT, too.

On the way to the mall, we passed the park, and saw Angeline again. But this time the kids looked entirely different from before. Obviously, her plastic surgeon dad had already started cutting the kids up to make perfect little miniature Angelines out of them.

Angeline's sick joy ←

Here's How those kids looked Before

Here's How they look now

We took Margaret around to the best stores at the mall. It was a little bit spiritual, because Margaret had not even heard of a lot of them. Isabella and I felt a little bit like we were doing something profound and wonderful, like teaching a gorilla sign language.

MARGARET
LIKE
MALL

Margaret started to chicken out a little at the clothes and accessories that Isabella and I had selected. She was craving some pencils pretty badly, but finally, she caved because we used **Peer Pressure** against her.

Bet I know what Margaret was thinking of

Adults think that Peer Pressure can influence what kids do, but it's actually a thousand times more powerful than that.

Obi-Wan Kenobi's Jedi mind tricks have nothing on Peer Pressure. Seriously. Isabella and I could have had Darth Vader in a miniskirt and braids in about five minutes.

We dropped Margaret off at Sally Winthorpe's house after the mall. I guess Sally had asked her over or something. (Maybe a Big Pencil Dinner.) But who cares? Because the main thing of the day or, as French people call it, *le main ting of ze day,* was **MY** new jeans! When we were at the mall, Mom found me a pair of **Bellazure Jeans.** They are the coolest jeans ever made and she bought them for me without my even having to ask. **Why did Mom buy me these really cool and really expensive pants??** I may never know.

But who cares?

The utter rapture of brand-
new jeans

Yeah, yeah. Mission accomplished with Margaret. She'll probably be a little bit better off. But now *I* own the coolest pair of jeans ever.

Stinker, I hope you are reading this, because I want you to know that an enraged girl can pick up a beagle by his fat little tail and hurl him directly into the core of the Sun if she is sufficiently antagonized, pants-wise.

so long, MUNCHY

Monday 16

Dear Dumb Diary,

    I wore my new jeans to school today, and I felt like I was the most beautiful bottom-half-of-a-girl on Earth. I was just getting ready to drink up all the compliments when Margaret walked into science class.

Aren't I adorable?

Then I heard something that I had never heard before. It's not a sound you often hear. It was sort of a soft, wet, popping sound. I realize now that it was the sound of twenty-six jaws dropping open at exactly the same time.

Margaret was, well, she was **GORGEOUS**. Her hair, her perfume, her jewelry, her new clothes, were working together like a symphony orchestra comprised of the rare supermodels who are smart enough to read music.

Margaret

Isabella and I took a little bit of pride in it, feeling sort of like the people who own those incredible dogs at dog shows. You know what I mean: We're not the dog, but without us the dog would be licking a fire hydrant somewhere instead of looking like a million bucks. (That's SEVEN million bucks in dog money.)

Note: Nobody is currently prepared to accuse Margaret of this sort of fire hydrant lickage.

Margaret was so happy. And Isabella was happy. And I was happy. And Hudson was happy. *(grrr!)*

And okay, I wasn't. There was something vaguely sinister in the air, and I'm not sure what it was.

Tuesday 17

Dear Dumb Diary,

Here's a peculiar scientific phenomenon I learned in class today and, like all of the important scientific discoveries, it involves choosing your deodorant wisely.

For instance, these choices not so good

Margaret borrowed my pencil today. She must have forgotten that she was no longer a Gerd, because when I looked up she had it in her mouth and was enjoying what could only be described as a *relationship* with it. It was one of those moments when you find yourself looking around for something to hit somebody with. (I have this moment about fifteen times a day.)

But then this soothing breeze of fragrant excellence comes wafting off Margaret and I felt, like, soothed. That is one excellent deodorant. I even let her keep eating my pencil.

But the soothery didn't last forever. Is soothery a word? Whatever. By lunch I was no longer soothed. And Isabella was visibly shaken.

Sure, she's always visibly shaken, but today, she was picking up a really strange vibe. Bad Mojo. Evil Juju.

Isabella, who is sharply attuned to this sort of thing, walked in and instantly observed that the precarious **Lunch Table Dynamic** had been upset.

She said that some of the Medium-Popular kids were sitting with the Less-Than-Medium-Popular kids. For a moment I thought she was nuts, until I saw Margaret was sitting at **THE ULTRA-MEGA-POPULAR** table. Isabella said this really should not happen. For Margaret to escalate that quickly, it could destroy the Natural Order of the Universe, and worse. . . .

ISABELLA FREAKS

Isabella said that it meant that we had fallen a notch. By accidentally inserting Margaret in at such a high level of popularity, we had actually pushed everybody below her down. She said we're suddenly tumbling into the Pit of Zero Popularity. Can she be right? Is there really such a thing as Popularity, or is it all some sort of weird scientific theory?

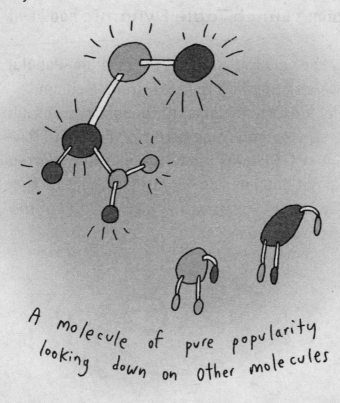

A molecule of pure popularity looking down on other molecules

Wednesday 18

Dear Dumb Diary,

    Wore the New Pants again. I didn't wear them yesterday, of course. You can't wear them **every** day, or people will say you only have one cool pair of pants, which they would be jerks for being right about.

    Thankfully, Stinker had not gone mental on them, but I don't know if that's because we are friends again, or because I've been hanging them in my closet where stubby little beagle legs can't reach.

PROBABLY STINKER'S GREATEST DREAM

so NOW he can have my pants as food

Long, elegant Legs

Isabella and I may have destroyed **The Entire Universe.** (I, for one, do not believe the Universe should be this fragile, because it's where I keep all my stuff.)

But here's what makes me think we destroyed it. Today at lunch, somebody was missing at the Mega-Popular table. Isabella was right. We did such a magnificent job on Margaret's makeover that she has bumped everybody. She has even bumped . . . Angeline!

It was a truly beautiful moment. **Angeline had been taken down a notch!** It was the most beautiful lunchtime moment since the time Miss Bruntford, the cafeteria monitor, slipped on a smear of creamed corn and gave an involuntary figure skating performance that ended with a double axel into a face-plant.

I love figure skating

But, just like *that* beautiful moment —
which was shattered by our having to stare at
Miss Bruntford's massive underpants until the
paramedics arrived (You're not allowed to move
somebody in that condition. We also learned
that tossing Tater Tots at her wasn't a good idea,
either.) — *this* beautiful moment was shattered by
the realization that if Angeline had been demoted,
then we were even lower than we thought.

TOWER OF POPULARITY

MOVIE STARS

CHIP

MARGARET

ANGELINE

HUDSON

ME

ISABELLA

SALLY

PICKERS OF NOSES

when we accidentally stuffed Margaret in here we destroyed the Universe and more important, Lowered our popularity

And Angeline was, in her typical deceptive way, not acting like it bothered her.

The pit of Unpopularity

As we were standing there alternately blaming each other for making over Margaret in the first place, we noticed Hudson walking over to the Mid-Popular table and, just as he did, my pants — How can I put this? — decided to *join the conversation.* You get my drift, Dumb Diary? My pants cut the cheese. Let one fly. Baked a batch of brownies. Got the picture?

I know what you're thinking, Dumb Diary, pants can't get gas. And yet . . .

Fortunately for me, Isabella, who comes from a large family and is therefore an expert on swiftly blaming others, pretended to be horrified by some confused innocent kid nearby. She made Hudson think that the noise came from **Confused Innocent Kid,** or **Stinkypants,** as I have learned since lunch that he has come to be called. By everyone.

Of course, I admire Isabella for being so good at getting others in trouble, but she didn't believe me when I told her that it was the pants all by themselves, and not me.

STINKY PANTS

ISABELLA'S
Big family
has taught her
how to efficiently
ruin the lives
of others
swiftly

Families are
the Best!

There's no **WAY** Isabella would have believed that the pants actually made me walk past the Mega-Popular Table, and that they also made me bump the table a little bit as if I was some sort of angry tough kid looking for trouble. Although now that I think about it, there's that one kid who actually bumps into *everything,* including lunch tables, and he's never looking for anything except his hat, which is routinely hidden from him.

What is with these pants, anyway?

Can PANTS make people think you are a huge DERF, like BUMP-into-everything KID?

Thursday 19

Dear Dumb Diary,

So tell me, Dumb Diary, if you were something small and ghastly, like a tiny, hairy creature that lived in a shower drain, and two beautiful fairy princesses took the time out from their very busy schedules to transform you into some sort of flying sparkling unicorn with diamond hooves that could shoot rainbow butterflies out its ears, would you just decide to throw it all away and cram yourself back into the shower drain?

HORRIBLE thing Re-crams itself

Well, that is exactly what Margaret did. She showed up today in science class without the new clothes, without the new jewelry, without the makeup.

ugly old hair

ugly old HAIR Accessory

ugly old clothes

ugly old beaver impersonation

ugly old shoe

ugly old other shoe

Isabella and I were floored. This meant that everything was back to normal. I accidentally let out this big cheer, and Mrs. Palmer dropped an alcohol burner, and then the whole room smelled like that substitute teacher who got fired last month for falling asleep in class.

Other Famous Substitute Teachers

— Mr. Stupid McClueless

The Sugar Substitute

The Tuna Sub

Of course, Mrs. Palmer employed her strategy of switching lab partners around. This means that now my lab partner is Mike Pinsetti, and Margaret is partnered up with some other kid, I forget who.

But I was so happy about Margaret's terrible judgment that this new partnerfication didn't really sink in.

In fact, as we switched seats, I even smiled at Mike Pinsetti, which made him try to smile back *(I think)*, but it looked more like he had his hand caught in a car door. I may be the first person who has ever smiled directly at Mike's face.

Yes, indeed, everything seemed pretty wonderful until lunch. That's when we saw IT.

PINSETTI TRIES TO PERFORM SMILING

Margaret was sitting at the Mega-Popular table, talking to Chip, in her old, pencil-eating-shower-drain-creature form. Even Sally Winthorpe seemed to take notice. It was as though the very **Wonderbread of Reality** had been besmeared by the Peanut Butter of Illusion, and further obscured by the Grape Jelly of — oh, I don't know, I'm trying to make it all relate to lunch.

The simple fact is that, according to Isabella, we're much, much lower on the Popularity scale now than ever before, since it appears that Margaret has ascended on her own *(yuck)* merits.

PUSH

Friday 20

Dear Dumb Diary,

Isabella came over tonight. She had some movie she had rented. (It was called *Terror at Your Throat*.) We started watching it, and it was about a haunted necklace and how bad things happened to this family after they got it. During the movie, Isabella jumped up and screamed that the necklace was exactly like my pants, which made Stinker commit Urine. It was probably because he is not used to people screaming while he is fast asleep. Still, I had to spank him a little for it.

Anyway, Isabella said it wasn't the makeover that boosted Margaret's Popularity and forced us down. It was the pants. She said it wasn't my loud "yahoo" in science that got me switched again so that I'm science partners with Known Goon, Mike Pinsetti. It was the pants. And she said it wasn't me who had done **you-know-what** all over Hudson Rivers. **IT WAS THE PANTS.**

I pointed out that I hadn't exactly gassed all over him. A debate followed, but she was firm on this point: The pants were to blame. **THE PANTS ARE HAUNTED.**

THE PANTS ARE HAUNTED

STARRING JAMIE KELLY AS THE HOT CHICK WITH THE COMPLICATED HAIR AND ISABELLA WHO IS NOT AS HOT INTRODUCING ANGELINE AS THE MUTANT GARGOYLE

STRANGE THINGS MY

WATCH 20-MINUTE COMMERCIAL ABOUT A CHICKEN ROASTER

TASTE KIWI SHAMPOO TO SEE if it's as good as it smells

CALL HUDSON AND HANG UP. THIRTY TIMES.

PANTS MADE ME DO

imagine TRAGIC EVENT IN WHICH everybody I know dies and I have to carry on prettily.

STROKE Roof of mouth with toothbrush and cause four-hour tickle.

Right now, Isabella is calling her mom to get permission to sleep over. I don't think I want to be in my room alone with the pants all night, and we plan to drive the spirits away tomorrow.

Saturday 21

Dear Dumb Diary,

    Isabella's first idea was to tear the pants to shreds. But I wanted to see if we could just drive the wicked spirits out of them without the rippage. I mean, c'mon. They *were* pretty cool pants after all.

Isabella's next idea was to use a Ouija board to contact the tormented ghosts in my pants, but I don't have a Ouija board, so we tried to do it with a Monopoly game. Sadly, we didn't really make much progress, except we decided to try to make charm bracelets with the dog and race car pieces.

More Glamorous Jewelry From Old Games

Lovely String of Pearls made from balls out of Hungry Hungry Hippos™ Game

Spooky Voodoo Necklace made from old Operation™ Game Bones

Pierced earrings made from Mr. Potato Head's™ Ears

I thought we should light candles and speak some sort of mystic chant. We're not really well-informed on chants, so we said the Pledge of Allegiance, which, though technically speaking is not a mystic chant, still sounds pretty creepy when you say it low and zombie-like in a dark room with flashlights. (Dad doesn't allow lit candles in my room, so we had to make do.)

Freaked ourselves out a little

84

Finally, we decided to just pound the evil out of the pants, and this took the form of laying the pants out in the backyard and stomping all over them in various evil-destroying karate-like moves. It occurred to us both at the exact same time just how dumb we looked, so we took them inside and stuffed them into the washing machine. They were torn up pretty good. Maybe all it will take now is a little sudsing.

The point when we thought we might not be banishing evil and we might be huge spazzes.

Sunday 22

Dear Dumb Diary,

   We walked to Isabella's house this morning, and when we passed the park we saw Angeline again. It looked like her dad had Plastic-Surgeoned those little kids back to their original appearances. Why would somebody do that? You can't just scribble out a plastic surgery and start over.
   Or can you?

Late-breaking Thoughts

Could there be another, simpler explanation? I asked Isabella, and she said no. She said that the most obvious answer was that Angeline's plastic-surgeon father was doing and undoing operations on her younger sisters in order to make them look like different kids on alternating weekends. Also, it appeared that he had some sort of way to change their heights.

START   CHANGED   CHANGED   CHANGED AGAIN
BACK

You have to hand it to Isabella. When she's right, she's right.

When I got home, I peeked in the washing machine and the pants were gone. Hmm . . . **Demon Pants** mysteriously vanished. The only reasonable thing to do was to run screaming upstairs to my room.

Other times when screaming is necessary...

Monster is chasing you and your high heels are too cute to abandon

Eaten by Ants

Gramps accidentally shoots a moon

Monday 23

Dear Dumb Diary,

THE PANTS ARE BACK. This morning when I woke up, there they were, hanging on a hanger, looking brand-new, and totally haunted. They had mysteriously healed themselves. Also, I think they were staring at me.

I moved slowly and carefully around the jeans and reached into my drawer for another pair, only to discover that Stinker had chewed one of his big round holes in my last pair of non-evil jeans.

No jeans left! I was so angry that I dropped everything and made a big sign. It says, "Have You Been Mean to Your Beagle Today?" in glitter. **GLITTER,** Stinker. That means I *really, really* mean it. People use glitter on signs only when they are dead serious. And I put it up on my wall where he could see it all the time.

Before I left for school, I cut up four hot dogs (possibly Stinker's favorite food) and put them in Stinker's dish. Then after he got a good look at them, I threw them out in the yard so that Stinker could sit by the window all day and watch the neighbor's cats sit out there and eat his hot dogs.

Tuesday 24

Dear Dumb Diary,

Margaret continues to travel in the Mega-Popular circle in spite of her undeniable Gerdness (or would it be Gerditude?). The Evil of the Pants is strong. Indeed, they are twisting the very fiber of our Universe. Up is down, left is right, over there is over there now (I'm pointing).

Haunted By the Demon Denim

Isabella says our only hope is plastic surgery. She says that if we can get Angeline's dad to do some work on us, we might be able to claw our way back out of the Unpopularity pit.

pit-clawing
is just
murder on
the nails →

I suppose it only makes good sense that you can feel better about yourself by letting somebody cut up your face, but I'm not sure exactly how that works. Isabella assured me that if we don't like what Angeline's dad does, he can always change us back like he does on Angeline's ever-changing little sisters. I guess I should consider it.

I told Isabella to ask Sally Winthorpe what she thinks, since she had offered to help Isabella and Margaret with their science homework after school.

Isabella says that Plastic Surgery makes you Beautiful

I just noticed my "Be Mean to Your Beagle" sign again.

I took Stinker into the bathroom and weighed him on the scale and told him that he was twenty pounds overweight.

I really don't want to be mean to Stinker anymore, but he has to learn his lesson.

Have a seat, Tubby

Wednesday 25

Dear Dumb Diary,

The pants are stronger than we thought. Even wadded up in the bottom of my closet, they still exert a destructive force at school, and here's how:

Margaret and Isabella's science homework was **WRONG.** Sally is never wrong. The only explanation is evil, jinxed jeans. Mrs. Palmer, like always, did a partner switch, and this time she put Sally and Hudson together, which seemed to make Sally sort of happy. (If I didn't know better, I would swear she was crushing on him a little. Do smart girls do that? I have no idea.)

Can a smart girl Have a crush?

OR WOULD SHe Have a BRaiN WHeRe HeR HeART SHouLD Be?

After school, Isabella made me help her corner Angeline. You are not going to believe how **WEIRD** this turned out to be, Dumb Diary.

Isabella is pretty blunt, so she just comes out and asks Angeline if her rich doctor dad will do plastic surgery on us.

Angeline looked pretty puzzled. She said that her dad worked in an office. He's an accountant.

I asked what about the little sisters we see her with in the park. Her dad keeps doing plastic surgery on them.

Those aren't her sisters. Those are kids she babysits. And they don't keep changing. They're different kids.

I know what you're thinking, Dumb Diary: Why does a rich girl need to babysit?

It turns out that Angeline is **NOT RICH.** She babysits because she needs to. She's saving up to buy — get this — a pair of Bellazure Jeans.

Angeline wants me to believe the lies
I keep telling about her

But none of that is the weird part. Here's the weird part: Angeline and I wear the exact same size jeans. How can that be? She looks like a Greek statue, and I look like the place where somebody started to carve a girl and then gave up halfway through the project.

we wear the same size? I didn't know we were even the same species.

Isabella offered to sell Angeline my jeans at half price and Angeline said okay. (Not a big surprise, really, that Isabella would make that move. Once, Isabella tried to sell somebody my shoes, and I was wearing them at the time.)

I started to tell Angeline that they were possessed by some sort of horrible otherworldly force, and Isabella gave me an elbow in the ribs. I just had to tell Angeline after finding out she was my **size-sister.**

She didn't care. She said she didn't believe in otherworldly forces. It's your funeral, Angeline.

Otherwordly Garment Spookiness

HAUNTED PANTS
(I CAN PROVE THESE)

POSSESSED UNDERWEAR
(THESE SEEM LIKELY)

VOODOO MUUMUU,
(I HOPE THESE EXIST. IT'S A GOOD RHYME)

Thursday 26

Dear Dumb Diary,

What a day. What a day.

Mom came in and woke me up for school and noticed my anti-beagle sign. I explained to her what Stinker had been doing to my jeans, but that I was getting tired of being mean to him, anyway, and would probably take it down soon. I was thinking of replacing it with a gentler sign saying, "Be Mean to Your Beagle When He Deserves It." Also, I was planning to diminish the imposing threat of the message through the use of less glitter.

Mom may have noticed where a Beagle's Face was mushed into the sign

Then Mom dropped her bomb. Stinker had **NOT** made those holes.

After our little discussion about clothing a few weeks ago, Mom had decided to try to "get with it." She found out that the lighter-blue denim was the cool jean of the moment, and she looked through my magazines for tips on bleaching jeans. She couldn't find any, so she decided to just give it a whirl on her own.

I love
my
mom

But
she's...

you
know...

ALL

MOMMISH

She had spilled some bleach on my jeans the first time, and it turns out that bleach can eat a big round hole right through a pair of pants. She tried a couple more times, but those were not any better, you'll remember. She felt so bad she bought me the Bellazure Jeans.

Ah, **GUILT.** And some people say it's a bad thing.

Later, my mom found the Bellazure Jeans that Isabella and I had destroyed in the washing machine on Sunday. Not knowing that Isabella and I had attempted to stomp the Evil out of them, Mom assumed that SHE was responsible for wrecking them in the wash. She rushed to the mall and bought a brand-new pair, which she hung on a hanger in my room. (So they *didn't* mysteriously heal themselves.)

I looked over at Stinker, who was listening to all of this with what could only be described as a scowl, even though I'm not sure a dog *can* scowl with lips that are pretty much just flaps.

I wonder if dogs can hold a grudge.

Isabella's sinus problem cleared up. Why is that worth mentioning? The day got weirder. You'll see, Dumb Diary.

ISABELLA'S NOSE FINALLY DOES SOMETHING

In science class today, I noticed that Margaret seemed a little more, I don't know, Gerd-like.

I also noticed that Hudson and Sally Winthorpe, the brand-new lab partners, were really chatting it up. I mean, **BIG-TIME.** They were laughing and smiling, and it was like they were the only two people in the room.

HUDSON

SALLY

The evil of the pants is indeed powerful

Then Sally flashed a quick glance my way, and I saw something in her eyes: **GUILT.** I recognized it as exactly the same precise expression that Stinker had not had about the pants, but Mom had.

When Isabella passed by Sally, she stopped for a second, and I could tell she was confused by something. And it was more than Isabella's normal confused look.

SALLY

CONFUSED LOOK →

SCIENCE

Other normal confused looks

Science class was the same as ever: chemicals this and chemicals that. When the bell rang, I went out into the hall, and Angeline strolled up to me. She wanted the pants, and I pulled them out of my backpack and handed them to her. She dashed to the bathroom to try them on.

From inside the science room, I heard Isabella and Sally Winthorpe squawking about something. Then I heard a jar break, and the fire alarm went off.

Everybody in the whole school filed outside,
and Isabella dragged Sally over to talk to me.

Isabella is probably tough
enough to be a girl bully (A GULLY)

Isabella said, "I was right. Tell her, Sally."

And Sally Winthorpe, smartest girl in my grade (maybe the school) explained:

Sally had taken an interest in Isabella's **Top Secret SuperFragrance** project. She was the one who had taken Isabella's jarful of concentrated perfume samples. And she had done it for . . .

DRAMATIZATION OF CRIME SCENE

Sally had a crush on him. She had been convinced by discussions with Isabella that Isabella's theory of **Unseen Levels of Popularity** was right. Based on that hypothesis, Sally believed that she had to make room in the middle if she was ever going to be on the same level as Hudson.

EVIL GENIUSES LIKE SALLY ARE AFTER WORLD DOMINATION OR GUYS

So Sally used Isabella's powerful perfume concoction on Margaret by sneaking some into Margaret's backpack when she had gone over to her house to study. The **SuperFragrance** was so totally incredibly complex and enticing that it actually increased Margaret's Popularity, even after she abandoned the other makeover stuff and became the shower drain creature again.

That increase in Margaret's Popularity subsequently lowered Isabella's and mine.

CRUNCH CHEW

perfume Hidden in Backpack

MARGARET'S BEAVER-GIRL DROPPINGS

Then all Sally, evil homely genius, had to do was make sure that Isabella and Margaret did their homework wrong and hope that Hudson would wind up with her after one of Mrs. Palmer's predictable partner switches. And he did!

At that point, Sally started using the SuperFragrance on herself, thereby hypnotizing Hudson with the fragrance, which I had found so soothing that I let Margaret eat my pencil.

I was **not** amazed to learn how smart Sally is

I was amazed to learn that smartness is good for something

And she would have gotten away with it, too, if Isabella's sinuses hadn't cleared up. Isabella smelled the distinctive SuperFragrance as she passed Sally's desk. Right after class, Isabella jumped (Isabella said, "leaped like a cat," but I've seen her play volleyball. Trust me: I was being charitable when I said "jumped.") and snatched the jar out of Sally's backpack.

They fought over it, it fell and broke open, and Mrs. Palmer, overcome by the fumes, tripped the alarm, thinking it was some sort of chemical accident. (This would have been worth seeing. Like all girls from big families, Isabella is good at fighting. One time, when one of her big brothers was picking on her, Isabella slapped him so hard that he couldn't taste anything for three weeks. Sally never had a chance.)

It was a total Scooby-Doo moment. Except for the fact that my dog is sort of a reject, and we can't put Sally in jail. But we *are* meddling kids. You have to give us that.

Yup, it all felt pretty good until Hudson walked up and swept Sally away. She shot a glance back at us as if to say, "So what? I *still* got my way, and you're still on the bottom." And she was right. The entire Universe was still just plain wrong.

Behold the Scent of Evil

POOR DUMB HUDSON

Which smells pretty good actually

And then, **IT happened.** I looked up and I saw Angeline coming out of the school. She had been changing in the bathroom when the fire alarm went off. Everybody in the school was outside. And when she opened the door, they all looked. It was the grandest entrance ever made, even though technically, it was an exit.

Angeline was wearing the Bellazure Jeans. But she was walking (I don't know how she does this) in slow motion. Even her hair was blowing in slow motion. Every eye in the school was glued on Angeline and the jeans and the knees of the jeans, which had holes in them.

← This is Beagle's work!

Stinker! These weren't Mom's perfect round
bleach holes; these were the irregular holes gnawed
by a mean little dog: rough, scraggly, thready
holes. WHY, STINKER? WHY?

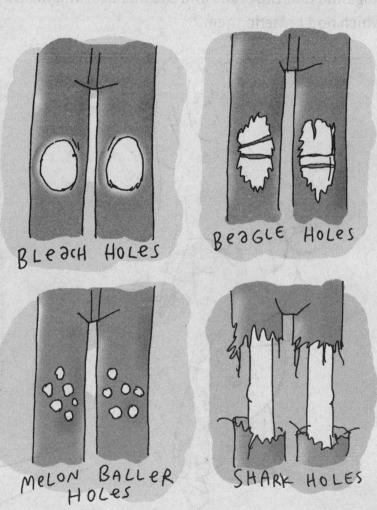

BLEACH HOLES

BEAGLE HOLES

MELON BALLER
HOLES

SHARK HOLES

Suddenly, I understood why. It was clear to me that it was because I told Stinker he was twenty pounds overweight. In dog weight, that's **140 POUNDS.** No wonder he was angry. Nobody wants to be told that they are 140 pounds overweight. The jeans were ruined.

But then I saw — we all saw — Angeline's kneecaps peeking out through the openings. It turns out that her knees look more like little tiny perfect bald angel heads than knees.

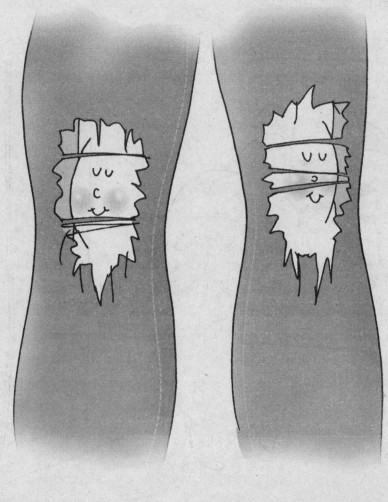

Angeline had just set a trend. Or maybe Stinker had. Either way, fragrance suddenly meant nothing to anyone. We all knew that how people smelled didn't matter, as long as they had jeans like Angeline's.

Angeline had regained her rightful position among the Mega-Populars. And Isabella said that it was like the spell of Margaret's makeover, the SuperFragrance, and the haunted pants had been broken.

Angeline walked over and handed me the money for the jeans. "I'll take 'em," she said.

And then Chip, King of Guys, and Hudson (who had abandoned Sally somewhere) walked up next to Angeline.

"Cool pants," Chip said.

Angeline looked right at me. A lot of things could have happened at that moment. She could have said almost anything.

What she did say was, "Thanks," pointing at Isabella and me. "These two designed 'em."

small feminine heart attacks

Friday 27

Dear Dumb Diary,

    Science class was, well, quiet today. Half the kids had on torn jeans, except for Mike Pinsetti, who had torn the elbows out of his sweatshirt. (Not a bad try, for him.)

    Isabella was more at peace than I've seen her in weeks. The pants had not been haunted, and the Universe seemed to be in balance again. The true Popularity Order had been restored. Also, Isabella

took some delight in pointing out that now it was absolutely clear that the pants themselves had not **Cut One** in front of Hudson.

It was me. (I blame Mom's cooking.)

Margaret was just happily enjoying pencil after pencil.

Sally didn't look quite so smart anymore, but Isabella and I decided to keep this to ourselves. Isabella says that we had a massive Popularity boost that brought us back up to normal, and maybe even slightly higher, thanks to Angeline. Besides, Sally was just after what we're all after.

Except for Angeline, who already has it.

Anyway, thanks for listening, Dumb Diary. I gotta go. I just remembered there's somebody I owe four hot dogs.

Jamie Kelly

Think you can handle another Jamie Kelly diary? Then check out

Dear Dumb Diary,

I got another poem today from You‑Know‑Who...

She is the fairest blossom, true,
She blooms in any weather.
But I must love her from afar.
We'll never be together.

Signed, M.P.

Can you believe the pain he's in? His suffering? The crushing heartache he endures every time he sees me? Gosh, it just makes me so happy!